The Ladybird Key W
based on these comr
used most often in t
introduced first—with
appeal to children. All the Key Words list is
covered in the early books, and the later titles
use further word lists to develop full reading
fluency. The total number of different words
which will be learned in the complete reading
scheme is nearly two thousand. The gradual
introduction of these words, frequent repetition
and complete 'carry-over' from book to book,
will ensure rapid learning.

The full-colour illustrations have been designed
to create a desirable attitude towards learning—
by making every child *eager* to read each title.
Thus this attractive reading scheme embraces
not only the latest findings in word frequency,
but also the natural interests and activities of
happy children.

Each book contains a list of the new words
introduced.

*W. MURRAY, the author of the Ladybird Key Words
Reading Scheme, is an experienced headmaster, author
and lecturer on the teaching of reading. He is co-author,
with J. McNally, of 'Key Words to Literacy'—a teacher's
book published by The Schoolmaster Publishing Co. Ltd.*

THE LADYBIRD KEY WORDS READING SCHEME has 12 graded books in each of its three series—'a', 'b' and 'c'. As explained in the handbook 'Teaching Reading', these 36 graded books are all written on a controlled vocabulary, and take the learner from the earliest stages of reading to reading fluency.

The 'a' series gradually introduces and repeats new words. The parallel 'b' series gives the needed further repetition of these words at each stage, but in different context and with different illustrations.

The 'c' series is also parallel to the 'a' series, and supplies the necessary link with writing and phonic training.

An illustrated booklet—'Notes for Teachers'—can be obtained free from the publishers. This booklet fully explains the Key Words principle and the Ladybird Key Words Reading Scheme. It also includes information on the reading books, work books and apparatus available, and such details as the vocabulary loading and reading ages of all books.

BOOK 4b
The Ladybird Key Words Reading Scheme

Fun at the farm

by W. MURRAY
with illustrations
by J. H. WINGFIELD

Publishers: Ladybird Books Ltd . Loughborough
© Ladybird Books Ltd (formerly Wills & Hepworth Ltd) 1965
Printed in England

Here are Jane and Peter at the farm. They like to come here to work, and they like to come here to play.

They want to help the man at the farm.

"We like to help you," says Peter to the man. "Yes," says Jane, "we have come to help."

"Good," says the man. "I want you to help me with the work."

---

farm   work

"Get some flowers for the house,"
says the man, "and then help with
the work in the house."

Peter and Jane get some flowers
and then go into the house.

They work in the farm house and
then they have some apples.

The man comes in to see Peter
and Jane. He says they can play.

Peter wants to see the farm dog

house   then

"Here is the dog," says Peter.

"Good dog," says Jane.

"He wants some water," says Peter. "Let us give him some."

They get some water for the dog.

"Look," says Jane. "He wants to come with us. Let him come, Peter. Let him come with us."

The dog jumps up and down. He likes to play with Peter and Jane, and he likes to look for rabbits.

let   us   him

Here are the boy and the girl with the farm dog. They go to look at the cows.

"I like the cows," says Jane.

"Yes, they give us milk," says Peter.

Jane says, "I like milk and you like milk."

"The dog likes water," says Peter.

They see a cow go into the water.

Then Peter says, "Let us go to see the horses."

---

cows   milk   horses

The two children see the two farm horses. They are not at work.

Then the horses look up and see the children.

"Look," says Jane. "Here they come. Here come the two horses."

Peter says, "They like us. They like children. Do not let the dog jump up."

"No," says Jane. "Do not let him jump up and down. Horses do not like it."

---

two   children   not   do

Peter has some apples. Jane says, "Give me some, please."

Peter gives two apples to Jane.

Then he gives the big horse an apple. "Look, Jane," he says, "the big horse likes this."

Jane gives the little horse an apple.

"Yes," she says, "and the little horse likes apples."

"I want to get on the big one," says Peter. "Help me up, Jane."

She helps Peter up.

---

big   little   she

Peter is on the big horse. He says, "Look at me, Jane. Away I go."

Jane says, "I will come with you."

She gets up on the little horse.

"Away I go," she says.

"Do not make the little horse jump," Peter says.

"No," says Jane, "I will not make him jump."

The dog sees the two children on the horses. He wants to look for rabbits

Away   away   will   make

Here are some rabbits. There are big ones, and there are little ones. The little ones like to play. They like to jump.

Peter and Jane can see the rabbits. The rabbits can not see the boy and the girl.

Then the rabbits see the dog and away they go.

"Off they go," says Jane.

"Yes," says Peter. "Off they go, and off we go."

---

there   off

The two children and the dog can see some water. The dog wants to go into the water, and Peter wants to look for fish.

Then they come to the water.

"Look, DANGER," says Jane. "It says DANGER."

"Keep away, Peter," she says, "Do not go there."

"Yes," says Peter, "I can see that it says DANGER. We can not go there. I will keep the dog away."

DANGER   keep

The man on the farm lets the two children help him. They want to work with him.

"I like it up here," says Peter.

"Yes," says Jane, "it is fun."

"Look at the dog," she says, "he wants to come up with us."

Peter looks down at the dog. "Yes, he wants to be up here," he says.

"Good dog," says Jane, "we will come down."

be

The man at the farm lets the children play.

"Let us make a little play house with this," says Jane.

"Yes," says Peter. "It will be fun. There will be no danger."

Then he says, "We will not make a little house, we will make a big one to play in. Then you and I, and the dog can get in it."

"Good," says Jane.

Peter says, "Yes, that is what we
will do. We will make a big play
house."

Jane helps Peter, and the dog
looks on.

Then the dog gets up with Peter.

"What do you want?" says Peter.

"He wants to play," says Jane.

"Keep off," Peter says to the
dog. "Do keep away."

"Be a good dog," says Jane.

Then the dog sees the farm cat.

---

what   cat

The farm cat likes children. She comes to Jane, and then she looks into the play house.

The dog comes down to see the cat. He likes the cat.

Jane and Peter go into the house. They put some things in the house for play.

"This is fun," says Jane. "I like this."

The dog comes into the play house with the two children.

---

put   things

"Come and see this, Peter," says Jane. "Do come and look at this. It is the farm cat. Look what she has."

"What fun," says Peter. "Will she let us play with her?"

"We will get her some milk," says Jane.

They go up to the farm to get some cow's milk for the cat. They give the milk to the cat and then they play with her.

---

her

Peter and Jane want to see the cows give milk.

"Here is the man with all the cows," says Jane.

"He will let us go in with him," says Peter. "He will let us see him milk."

They all go in with the cows.

Then the man works and Peter and Jane look on.

"The cows are good," says Peter.

"Yes," says Jane, "they all like to give milk."

all

The children help with the work.
They help the man at the station.

He thanks Peter and Jane, and
gives the children some sweets.

Then they go to a shop for some
tea.

In the shop Peter has some cakes
and Jane has some milk.

"It was fun at the station," says
Peter. "I like to see the trains."

They thank the man for the tea.

---

thanks

The children play games at the farm.

Peter is up a big tree. He has a ball and plays a game with the cat. She jumps for the ball.

Jane says, "I want to draw. I will draw here."

"Come on, Peter," she says, "let us draw."

She draws a house.

"Look, Peter," she says, "this house is on fire."

She makes the fire red.

games   draw   fire

Jane has a game with the farm cat.

"I want you to be my cat," she says. "I want you to come to my home with me. My Daddy and Mummy like cats."

Peter draws. He draws a bus and a Police car. Then he draws a man.

"Look, Jane," he says. "I can make this man put some water on the fire. He will stop the fire."

---

my   stop

"What do you want to do?" says Jane to Peter.

"I want to play with my boat or the water," he says.

"Come on, then," says Jane. "Let us go and get the boats and play."

Peter gets his toy boat. His boat is a big one. Jane gets her boat. Her boat is a little one.

They go off to the water with the boats.

his

Peter and Jane come to the water. They put the boats on the water.

"It is fun to play like this," says Peter.

The dog wants a game. He wants to be in the water with the two children.

"Do not let him jump in," says Jane. "Stop him, stop him, Peter."

"Good dog," says Peter. "You come here. Here you are, you can have this ball."

They put all the play things away
and go into the farm house.

The man is there. He has a little
girl. She is not at the farm. She is
away at the sea with her Mummy.
Her Daddy can not go to the sea.
He has to work on his farm.

He thanks Peter and Jane for
the help, and then gives the children
a good tea.

sea

"Here is Daddy with the car,"
says Peter. "He has come for us. We
have to go home."

"Look," says Jane. "Pat is here.
Pat is in the car."

"Thank you for the tea," says
Peter to the man.

"Yes, thank you," says Jane.

Peter puts all his things in the
car. Jane has some flowers for
Mummy.

They get into the car with Daddy
and Pat.

They are all in the car.

"We are off," says Peter.

They see shops, and then the school.

"Do you like to play, or to go to school?" says Jane to Peter.

"I like work or play," says Peter.

"We all read at school," says Jane. "I like to read."

"I like to read at home or at school," says Peter.

"Yes, we all read at home," says Daddy.

---

or read

Daddy reads and Mummy works

Peter and Jane help Mummy. They water the flowers and put the play things away.

They like to help in the home.

Mummy gets some milk for Peter and Jane.

"Here you are," she says. "Have this, and then you have to go to bed."

"Can we have some apples, please?" says Peter.

"Yes," says Mummy. "Apples do you good."

New words used in this book

Total number of new words 41

The vocabulary of this book is the same as that of the parallel reader 4a.